All the World
a Poem

by Gilles Tibo
Illustrations by Manon Gauthier
Translation by Erin Woods

pajamapress

First published in Canada and the United States in 2016
Text copyright © 2016 Gilles Tibo
Illustration copyright © 2016 Manon Gauthier
This edition copyright © 2016 Pajama Press Inc.
Translated from French by Erin Woods
Originally published in French by éditions de l'Isatis
10 9 8 7 6 5 4 3 2 1

www.pajamapress.ca   info@pajamapress.ca

 Canada Council   Conseil des arts
for the Arts   du Canada

 ONTARIO ARTS COUNCIL
CONSEIL DES ARTS DE L'ONTARIO
an Ontario government agency
un organisme du gouvernement de l'Ontario

Canadä

The publisher gratefully acknowledges the support of the Canada Council for the Arts and the Ontario Arts Council for its publishing program. We acknowledge the financial support of the Government of Canada through the Canada Book Fund (CBF) for our publishing activities.

Library and Archives Canada Cataloguing in Publication

Tibo, Gilles, 1951- [Poésies pour la vie. English]
All the world a poem / by Gilles Tibo ; illustrations by
Manon Gauthier ; translation by Erin Woods.
Translation of: Poésies pour la vie. Poems.
ISBN 978-1-77278-009-3 (hardback)
I. Gauthier, Manon, 1959-, illustrator II. Woods, Erin,
1989-, translator III. Title. IV. Title: Poésies pour la vie. English
PS8589.I26P6313 2016   jC841'.54   C2016-901736-2

Publisher Cataloging-in-Publication Data (U.S.)

Names: Tibo, Gilles, author. | Gauthier, Manon , illustrator. | Woods, Erin, translator.
Title: All the world a poem / by Gilles Tibo ; illustrations by Manon Gauthier ; translation by Erin Woods.
Description: Toronto, Ontario Canada : Pajama Press, 2016. | Originally published in French by éditions de l'Isatis, Montreal, as Poésies pour la vie. | Summary: "A wonder-filled tribute to poetry in which verses of many styles celebrate the acts of writing, reading, and experiencing poems"— Provided by publisher.
Identifiers: ISBN 978-1-77278-009-3 (hardcover)
Subjects: LCSH: Children's poetry, Canadian. | BISAC: JUVENILE FICTION / Poetry. | JUVENILE FICTION / Concepts / Words. | JUVENILE FICTION / Imagination & Play.
Classification: LCC PR9199.3T536 |DDC 811.54 – dc23

Original art created with paper collage and mixed media
Manufactured by Transcontinental Printing. Printed in Canada

Pajama Press Inc.
181 Carlaw Ave. Suite 207 Toronto, Ontario Canada, M4M 2S1

Distributed in Canada by UTP Distribution
5201 Dufferin Street Toronto, Ontario Canada, M3H 5T8

Distributed in the U.S. by Ingram Publisher Services
1 Ingram Blvd. La Vergne, TN 37086, USA

For Claire Dion, and all the poetry that we inhabit.
G.T.

For Mr. Kang Woo Hyon and his team.
For all the magic and poetry of Nami.
M.G.

I love poems sweet and silly.
I love poems long and frilly—
All the poems dreaming on the shelf.

Poems tall or short or wide—
All are infinite inside
And live to tell the world
about itself.

Day or night, with friend or foe,
I love poems even though
I haven't found a rhyme for "chocolate."

Poetry lives in books, yes,
but also in the stars,
on the moon,
in tree-branch tangles.

Anything the world can be
in nighttime hush or daytime glee
is poetry.

Poetry is:
Tossing a ball as high as the sun,
going fishing
under a rainbow sky,
a bicycle race
in summer's embrace,
chasing ladybugs and wishing
on one,
seeing the sea in each glass of water you pour
And loosening the sky to watch it soar...

I write a poem on the waves
And on the wind above—
Messages flying
To the ones I love.

A thousand kisses later,
The letter is sealed:
X O X O scattered
Like sheep in the field.

I write the sun to warm my heart.
I write the moon to light my dark.
I walk among the blooming words
On velvet feet that leave no mark.
And if I wrote a thousand stars,
Would dreams light up with every spark?

A poem has fallen from the sky,
slipping from a cloud.
A second has sprouted from the earth
like a rainbow flower.
A third floated in from the sea,
bobbing at the end of the big pier.
I gather up the three poems
and hold them to my heart.
Then I continue my journey
toward the endless country
of verses yet to come.

At night,
all the poems
from all the books
put on their pajamas
and curl up
under my quilt.
Impossible to sleep
when all these words hide
beneath my pillow,
or with all the songs
my teddies
hum.

I am a poet
in December,
November,
October,
September—
but never August.
In August I rest,
always dressed
in white, and caressed
by a wind from the west,
with one I love best
held close to my chest.

Poetry
is like a flower
that blooms
in the rain.
Poetry
is a mockingbird
that wings me away
to a land with no pain

Under the night sky,
I laugh and I cry.
I couldn't say why.
It's so lovely, so high:
A poem for the eye.

This night,
I write
Without light,
But the words shine bright.

To write *poetry*
is to pluck silence like a flower
and press it gently between the pages
of a notebook
made of light.

When silence creeps across the night,
I curl up in my bed to write
A poem to my love, my light
(His name is Jeremy).

And then, to see if it sounds nice,
I read the poem once or twice
To all the lovely, little mice
Who listen silently.

If I wrote you a poem on the back of a cat,
Would you laugh at that?

If I wrote you a poem on the wings of a bird,
Would you think me absurd?

If I wrote you a poem in the palm of my hand,
Would you understand?

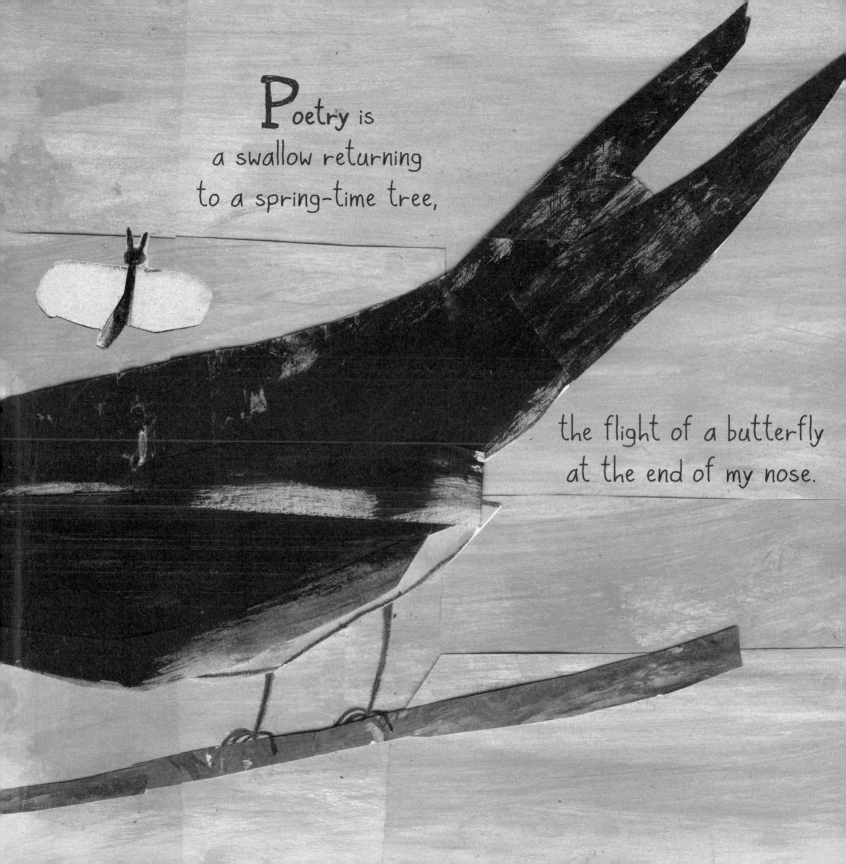

Poetry is
a swallow returning
to a spring-time tree,

the flight of a butterfly
at the end of my nose.

But
My favorite kind of poetry
Is this, my friend:
You, close to me.

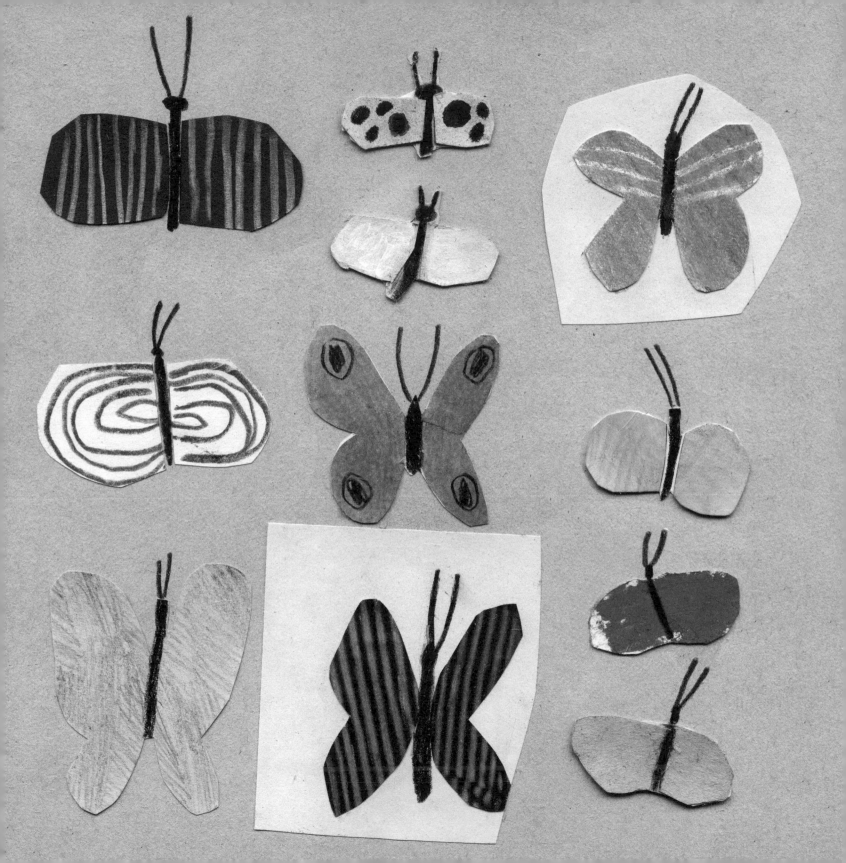